A VOYAGE TO
THE ISLAND OF THE ARTICOLES

By ANDRÉ MAUROIS

A Voyage to
THE ISLAND OF THE ARTICOLES
by
ANDRÉ MAUROIS

Translated from the French
by
·DAVID GARNETT

Wood engravings by
EDWARD CARRICK

D. APPLETON AND COMPANY
New York : : *Mcmxxix*

To

Madame la Comtesse

ANDRÉ DE FELS

AUTHOR'S NOTE

THE reader will be surprised to discover that
on page 59 Martin wrongly attributes to his
friend Snake the authorship of four lines of a
poem which is really by Rupert Brooke.

A VOYAGE TO
THE ISLAND OF THE ARTICOLES

A VOYAGE TO THE ISLAND
OF THE ARTICOLES

I

I ONLY wish to speak here of the Articoles and of their customs and of my adventures amongst them; I am keeping the story of what went before our arrival at their island for my big work, *The Pacific,* which will not be finished for two or three years yet. But that the reader may understand this fragment, it is essential that I should give a brief outline of how the voyage was undertaken.

My father, Jean Chambrelan, was a shipowner in a small way; I spent almost all my childhood with him at Fécamp and Etretat. My greatest pleasure was to go out with the fishermen in those old big-bellied boats which they call *caloges,* in those parts; that is how I acquired very young the instincts of a seaman. And by a seaman I mean a man who can navigate a

1

sailing ship and who can smell his way about in all weathers. In my eyes the modern seaman, on board a torpedo-boat or a steam-yacht, is nothing but an adventurous mechanic who drives a racing car out at sea.

My mates the fishermen had a high opinion of 'the young gentleman from Fécamp,' and amongst them I became dangerously accustomed to being treated with too much respect. When my parents sent me to school in Paris, where my Norman accent was made fun of, I took a dislike to my fellow-creatures at once. I was the lonely sort of schoolboy who prowls round the playground with his hands in his pockets and no friends. I needed sympathy, and my shyness stood in the way of my winning it.

Luckily the war caught me just as I was leaving school and threw me back into a way of living which suited my odd character. Danger, hardship, filthy shelters, the cold and the rain did not alarm me; what I feared was intimate contact with human beings.

I was soon an officer, and army discipline hedged me round with the framework I needed. A slight adventure put the finishing touch to my fear of people; I was wounded, and during my stay in hospital fell in love with a rather pretty nurse and wanted to marry her. She refused me. I got into the way of avoiding women's society during my leaves. The armistice and the peace were events which filled me with melancholy, as they did many young men. What was I going to do? I had not learned any trade. My father had died during the war and his ships had been sold; my only tastes were for a seaman's or a soldier's life. I tried staying in the army, but life in barracks is very different from campaigning. My wildness turned into a chronic state of highstrung nerves and everything in which my companions took delight seemed to me wearisome and idle. In 1922 I handed in my papers. My mother had just died leaving me a little money; I was thinking of emigrating to the colonies.

Just then a young Frenchman, Gerbault, crossed the Atlantic in a little 11-metre cutter, alone, and published the diary he kept on board. This came to me as a revelation. A single-handed voyage! That was what I was built for. Only I was more tempted by the Pacific than by the Atlantic. I had been a great reader of Stevenson, Schwob, and Conrad, and had always longed to see those islands with wonderful names: Butaritari, Apemama, Nonuti. The very word atoll enchanted me; I imagined a crystal diadem encircling a dark blue lagoon. Just as I feared an European woman with her coquettishness and her caprices, so I was attracted by what I believed primitive woman to be: a faithful, silent, sensual little animal.

In an hour I had made up my mind.

At the end of his book, Gerbault gave several pieces of practical advice to those who might wish to imitate him. In particular he described the type of boat and gave a list of stores and equipment. I drew up estimates and realized that I was in danger, unfortunately, of running short of money very quickly. My solicitor, with whom I discussed the position, advised me to go and see one or two of the big newspapers, and a publisher, and to obtain funds by publishing the account of my voyage. It was good advice, and I was able to sign two profitable contracts, to obtain advance payments and order my little boat to be built. It was a vessel of ten tons, entirely decked, and Bermuda rigged.

The newspaper with which I had contracted naturally wished to magnify the importance of

my expedition by announcing it beforehand to
its readers, and asked me for an article on my
plans. I described where I meant to go, and
throughout the following week I received the
most surprising letters sent on to me by the
newspaper. Most of my correspondents wished
to accompany me. I saw then how the state of
mind that I was in, a horror of social life and the
desire to escape from it, is far more common
to-day than anyone supposes. Several officers
of the Russian Navy, who had become taxi-
drivers or commissionaires in Paris, asked me to
let them go with me as my crew. Naturalists,
cinematograph operators, cooks in restaurants,
offered their services. But women especially im-
plored me to take them with me. 'I have been
so unhappy . . . I would be your slave . . .
I will stitch your sails, and cook your meals . . .
You shall treat me as a servant. I must leave
France, I must indeed,' said one. 'I saw your
photo in the newspaper,' wrote another candi-
date. 'You look unhappy, but gentle, and you
have lovely eyes.' This budget amused me, but
I had decided to go alone. Anne's letter was one
of the last. Even before I opened it I saw that
it had nothing in common with those I had re-

ceived. I liked the sober paper, the neat handwriting, the firmness of the characters. 'I do not know, Sir, if you are worthy of this letter, but I shall be able to judge by the tone of your answer, if you do answer it, which is unlikely. I have just read your article: you are going to do what I can but dream of. I have always loved the sea above all things: on land I dream of the smell of tar, the biting wind, the dollops of salt water smacking on the cabin sides—the Pacific islands. . . . Reading what you said, I thought that I heard my own thoughts spoken. Therefore I tell you: I am a widow, very young, fairly rich, completely free. I should like to go with you. Realize once and for all that I am not offering to be your bedmate, but your shipmate. I think that this is possible. I am certain to be useful to you. I know nothing of your qualities as a seaman; all my friends, some of whom are grim outspoken Englishmen, have recognized mine. You are necessary to me, you or some one else, because there are jobs requiring strength which unfortunately a woman has not got. As regards money: we shall share the cost of buying the boat, fitting her out, and the expenses of the voyage in equal halves. Possible bothers: None. I am alone in the world. Nobody will call you to account for what I do. Why do I write to you and not to one of my sailor friends? Because such adventures as yours are rarely met with, and also because the names of the poets you mention in your article are proofs that we have tastes in common. My address: 39 Quai Bourbon, Isle-St.-Louis. My telephone number: Gobelins 31–35. If you want to see me let me know, and I will meet you any day and time of day which suits you except Tuesday and Saturday morning when I attend classes at the Museum.'

Why did I reply? It was contrary to all my vows. The letter pleased me. There was something straightforward and manly in the style which reassured me. The name, Anne de Sauves, was pretty. 'Why not see her?' I asked myself, and already I was finding excuses for changing my plans. She undertook half the expenses: that made the voyage certain without worries about money, and rendered it possible to prolong it. There was plenty of accommodation on board considering the small size of the vessel. There would be no difficulty in putting up two bunks in it separated by a partition. When

I went to see Madame de Sauves I was already prepared to give in. The moment I saw her my mind was made up. She was not absolutely pretty, but her face had the pleasant and neat comeliness of her writing. Her voice was enchanting: even now after four years she seems to me the most genuine person I have ever met. With her not only did I never feel embarrassed, but the very notion of being ill at ease seemed absurd to me. She spoke of all things straight out, without finding circumlocutions and without hesitating. Moreover, our conversation was chiefly that of two seamen. After the first five minutes we began to sketch the sails and make lists of ships' stores.

Anne's idea was only to have two sails, mainsail and jib, and no bowsprit, but my boat was already on the stocks, and besides, with two of us, handling her would be easy. She was very much astonished to learn that I had ordered my boat to be built in France. The most convenient port of departure for a cruise in the Pacific was San Francisco. Why not have her built there from our plans? She had lots of friends in America and could get the work overlooked. This seemed to me sensible, and I promised to try to get the contract which I had entered into at Saint-Nazaire cancelled in a friendly way. Already I was speaking of 'our boat.'

I asked her to tell me something about her life. She had been brought up in the Vendée by a strict family who, without consulting her, had married her at eighteen to a neighbour, a very rich man, already old. During the war she had lost her husband and her nearest relatives. She had not been happy either as a girl or as a wife. 'But I don't want to pretend I'm a tragic case either. I've never been very unhappy: I've a sense of humour which always enables me during the worst moments to see the comic side of my unhappiness.' She liked to do things well. Everything in her house gave an impression of attention to detail. There was little furniture, but it was good. The walls were bare: there were no knick-knacks but many books. I noticed works on navigation, swimming and medicine. Her car was waiting at the door, and she brought me back to the centre of Paris herself; she drove well, quietly, without effort.

II

THE story of our voyage from San Francisco to Honolulu will, as I have said, find a place in another work. It is enough to note here that all went well on the trip. Our boat the *Allen* was a damned good sea-boat. At first we felt obliged to take the watch in turns, but we had soon realized that with the tiller lashed and sails fully reefed all night, we should find ourselves almost in our right course when we woke up. We ran into three storms, one of which was quite bad; Anne proved her mettle in the course of it.

She was, as I had foreseen ever since our first meeting, the ideal companion for a voyage. She was an excellent organizer, and it was she who in San Francisco bought all the stores we had on board and who, while we were afloat, cooked us our simple and wholesome meals. She did not know what it was to be ill-tempered.

10

In moments of danger her manner was natural, her movements neat. I used to call her 'Your Serene Highness.' With one accord we had fallen into an affectionate and familiar relationship. Anne wished neither to be courted nor to be protected; it may sound hackneyed to say that we lived together like brothers, yet the phrase gives the best picture of our relations. But to be accurate, I must add, that my feelings were more complicated; I often fancied I discovered longing and tenderness among them, but then I hastened to set to work and to think of something else.

From the Hawaiian islands it was my intention to go to Tahiti, but making a loop to see the Marquesas and the Touamatou islands in passing. Honolulu had disappointed me: an American Monte Carlo. It seemed to me that the great rings of white coral, glittering above the sea, would at last be something new to look at. About twenty days out from Honolulu I took our bearings, which showed me that we were 161·2° west longitude and 5·3° north latitude. We were therefore approaching the Fannings, a group of rocky, barren islands, but on which Findlay's Almanack says there is a British cable repair station; it was there that I counted on replenishing our supply of fresh water.

Towards evening we ran into a belt of dead calm with a rather big sea. Vicious little waves, whose tops broke in foam, began to beat on the *Allen's* bows in rapid, irregular rhythms. Then a breeze sprang up, which freshened rapidly and a great bar of clouds, black as ink, showed very low down on the horizon. Soon the wind became really strong and the *Allen* began to heel over. It was as hot as a boiler. We had already seen some bad squalls, but we realized at once that they had only been child's play compared with this one. The sky was now nothing but a race of black clouds, blown at full gallop by the wind. Immense waves broke on board; with each one the deck was under water. The sunken bulwarks swept through the sea.

Furling all the sails, and lashing the tiller amidships, we got a little respite, but we had to cling to the mast not to be swept overboard ourselves. Standing in the gale, with her hair flying, with a happy face and calm brow, Anne was splendid, a sea goddess. Towards midnight, when it was clear that we could do nothing, and the waves were running still higher, she said: 'Let's go and lie down.' Although the covers of the skylights were in place, everything was swimming in water down below, but we were so exhausted that, after pumping as best we could, we both fell asleep.

After some hours, a strange noise of violent blows striking the hull of the *Allen* awoke me. Was it day, or night? We could see nothing. The boat had a list, like the side of a roof; it was impossible to stand upright. I climbed on to the deck on all fours.

The clouds were so low, and so thick, that although it was daylight one could not see thirty yards. The waves were terrifying. Our bowsprit was smashed; it was that which was hammering on the side of the boat. Why had I not listened to Anne's advice when she had asked me to do without one! The panel of the sail locker had been torn off: the *Allen* was a mere wreck. I called Anne. I needed her help to cut adrift the bowsprit, which might make a hole in our hull. 'I think that we are lost,' I said to her. She drew a deep breath of the salty wind and smiled.

After an hour's work, during which I risked being carried overboard a score of times, I succeeded in cutting the bowsprit adrift. That

13

was one danger the less. Hot blinding rain beat on our faces and we went down once more into the cabin. Our clothes had been torn to bits in the course of this fearful task, but when Anne wished to change she found all our chests flooded. What was more serious, the instruments had been turned upside down. The chronometer could not be found; Anne's watch was smashed. Findlay's Almanack and the charts were a sodden mass of paper. Henceforward, if we survived the storm, we could not navigate the ship except by guesswork. Moreover, how could we sail her? We had lost our bowsprit, and our sails were in rags. Fortunately in the midst of these gloomy thoughts sleep once more wrapped us in her arms.

III

WHEN I opened my eyes I was startled by a strange impression of stillness and of silence; the *Allen* was rocking gently on an even keel. A peep of clear grey dawn showed through the hatchway. On deck, where I leapt in a single bound, a magnificent sight awaited me. In front of us the sun was rising in a saffron yellow sky. The wind had fallen; little golden and mauve clouds stretched in parallel banks through the warm air. The startling yellow of the sky was reflected in the sea which murmured gently round us.

'Anne!'

She ran up. I saw that beneath a blanket she was naked.

'Saved?' she asked me.

'We can't be sure yet.'

'How beautiful it is! Where are we?'

I reminded her that I no longer had any means

15

of knowing. God only knew how far the cy-
clone might have thrown us off our course.

'The sails?'

I showed them to her: she suggested trying
to make a mainsail with a blanket.

We were certainly near land, for birds were
flying round the boat. I sat down beside her
in the sunshine and we set to work. The strange
thing was that though perhaps we were doomed,
we were neither sad nor alarmed. On the contrary, we were both conscious of a feeling of
peace and gladness.

About noon I went below to try to find one
of the charts. When I returned empty-handed,
she said, 'Land,' and she showed me a dark short
line in the distance. It was an island, an island
with a dominating peak. But we were very far
from it. Climbing to the top of the mast, I
waved some linen rags for a long while. Luckily
the current was carrying us towards land: pres-
ently I could make out a cape, then a forest and,
it seemed to me, the shining roofs of a town.

'But how odd it is, Anne. It is a port. I see
something like a jetty. Where can we be? It
is not the Fanning Islands. There would be no

16

It was an island, an island with a dominating peak.

mountains, and I do not see what great town. . . .'

An hour later a skiff was coming out to us. As it approached we saw with surprise that it was manned by white sailors. I don't know why we expected a canoe . . . savages. . . .

Anne wrapped herself up better in her blanket. With one shoulder bare she was very pretty. At the bows of the skiff was a braided quartermaster, who called out in English: 'Who are you?'

'French, crossing the Pacific; we have suffered a good deal in last night's storm. Can we put in here for repairs?'

He seemed embarrassed, and said: 'It's not for me to decide that. The Commission. . . . You must come into port.'

I threw him a rope and asked him to tow us in. He suggested we should go on board of him, but I did not want to leave my boat; and Anne, naked beneath her blanket, did not want to be alone with the men. He took us in tow and led us towards the town. Anne and I asked each other to what country these men belonged. They did not wear the caps of English sailors, nor those of Americans.

'Australians?'

'No, I don't think so.'

At the stern of the skiff floated a strange flag, with nine women's faces on a white ground.

The port was small but natty. The pole, painted blue and white like the skiff, flew the white flag with nine faces, at the top of a mast.

Anne took hold of the tiller to come alongside whilst I tried to put a few things in a bag to take ashore; and we landed. Our rescuer led us under a shed and asked us what we wanted while waiting till the Commission could see us. Anne wanted a dress, and I a pair of trousers, and one of the men ran off in a hurry to the town.

I asked if there was a French Consul.

'No,' the Quartermaster answered. 'There are no consuls here. The island is private property.'

'Private property? But whose?'

'The Articoles.'

'But who are the Articoles?'

He began to speak again of the Commission. We could make nothing of it.

'Are you an Articole?' Anne asked him.

'Oh no,' he said, with a sort of modesty, as

19

though that were too flattering a supposition. 'Oh no, I am a Beos.'

'What a queer business. And the natives?'

'There are no natives.'

'But what is the island called?'

'It was formerly called Maiana; it is now the island of the Articoles.'

Just then the sailor came back with a parcel; he gave it to us, saluted, and retired discreetly. Anne threw off her blanket and put on the frock. It was made of a flimsy blue material, tied round the waist with a sash; in the parcel there was also a big yellow amber necklace.

'Look here,' she said to me. 'What a pretty attention! They are delightful, these unknown people!'

We tried to remember the names, Maiana, and the Articoles, but it did not seem as though either of us had ever heard them spoken of before.

IV

ON a little varnished wooden bungalow was a
plate engraved 'Temporary Immigration.' I expected to find a Customs-house smelling of to-
bacco and lined with notices; the room into
which we were shown was a delightful studio
with Morris chairs, upholstered in gay cretonnes
surrounding a table of some pale, polished wood.
Tea was served; an English country house tea,
pink cake, green cake, huge plum-cake, slices
of thin brown bread and butter. On the walls
there were shelves full of books. Three of the
arm-chairs were occupied by our judges, who
rose when we came in. The one on the left was
a little man of the moujik type with an untidy
beard, but with deep and gentle eyes; the one in
the centre, on the other hand, was very tall and
bald, with a clean-shaven, almost Japanese face,
intelligent and rather hard; the one on the right
was much younger than the other two. He

21

seemed an ethereal being, ready to fly away. His hair was a mist of flaxen curls and his eyes blue-grey. It was obviously the man in the centre who presided; to our surprise he spoke in French, in an agreeable, rather sing-song voice, and with curiously precious phrases.

'Let me introduce you,' said he, 'to my colleagues Routchko (the bristly little fellow) and Snake (the beautiful youth). My own name is Germain Martin, and I owe the honour of presiding at your examination to my having been born in France. However, it is as well that I should inform you at once that the literary language of this island is English. Will you be so kind as to tell me your names?'

'I am Pierre Chambrelan,' I said, 'and this is Madame de Sauves, my partner on this voyage: I don't know if you have received any French newspapers giving an account of our attempt to cross the Pacific. Three days ago our boat was completely crippled by the storm. We only want permission to put in here for repairs and then to continue our voyage. I have some money on board to pay for the expenses of refitting; if it should not be enough, Madame de Sauves

22

has an account with the Westminster Bank, and
I suppose that by cable . . .'

'My dear sir,' said Germain Martin in a bored
tone, 'please drop the question of money. The
subject is worn out. . . . Our Beos will repair
your boat, and will be only too happy to do so.
The only question which we, the Board of Temporary Immigration, have to decide is whether
you can be authorized to stay in the land of the
Articoles, or, on the other hand, if there is not
sufficient reason for us to detain you here for
some months.'

'Some months?' said I in alarm. 'But—'

'I beg you,' Martin broke in, with a kind of
playful authority, 'to wait. . . . You will see
that everything can be arranged. Madame, please
sit down. Will you have a cup of tea?'

Anne, who was dying of hunger, accepted
with joy. Snake helped her, and when we were
all comfortably seated, Martin went on: 'Let
us see. You are crossing the Pacific Ocean quite
by yourselves, in the little vessel which I was
able to look over just now. Can you tell us the
object of this surprising expedition?'

'Our only reasons were a love of the sea and
a horror of ordinary social existence. Both

23

Madame de Sauves and I felt the same need of escaping from civilization for some time. We were both good sailors, and we became partners for this cruise.'

Martin turned to each of his acolytes in turn with shining eyes. 'Most interesting,' said he with a long stress on the word 'most.'

Routchko fixed his beautiful eyes on mine in a long stare. 'My dear Mr. Chambrelan,' he said to me sympathetically, 'was Madame your mistress before you set out, or has she become your mistress since?"

Anne put her cup down on the table angrily. 'What a question!' she said. 'I am *not* his mistress. We are sailing partners, that's all, and what business is it of yours?'

Martin laughed; he had an astonishing laugh, childish and diabolic at the same time.

'My dear friend,' he said to Routchko, 'you must be patient. . . . But her tone was charming, wasn't it, Snake?'

'Yes,' answered Snake dreamily, 'so authentic. . . .'

'You must, my dear strangers, forgive our friend Routchko,' Martin went on. 'He believes that all mankind shares his own love of confession in public. But, and I must beg your pardon, his question was one which our duty, as Commissioners of Immigration, compels us to put to you. Speak without fear, for here you are in a land which is freed from all conventional morality. If you are lovers we shall take note of the fact, but we shall be very far from censuring you for it. Quite the contrary,' he added with a new and strange intonation.

'I am speaking without the slightest fear,' I said then. 'But what Madame de Sauves said is the truth. We are only shipmates.'

'What!' exclaimed Routchko. 'You've lived side by side on this boat alone, and far from the control of society, and your desires have not proved stronger than your pride? It is a perfect case,' he added in a low voice, turning towards Martin.

'*Most* interesting!' said Martin. 'I believe, my dear colleagues, that further questioning might spoil the psychological possibilities of the specimen. I propose referring the case to the Psycharium.'

'Approved,' said Routchko, giving us a tender look.

'And you, Snake?' asked Martin.

25

But Snake for the last minute or two had been scribbling in a notebook and glancing at Anne from time to time. He sighed. 'Yes,' said he. 'The Psycharium, of course.'

'Then,' Martin wound up, 'dear guests, for from now onwards you are our guests, while they busy themselves, slowly, in repairing your ship, you shall be lodged in the central Psycharium of Maiana. You may go there with complete confidence. You will be treated there with kindness, you will find solid but sufficient comfort. We shall see you again there. Ah, I was forgetting, my dear colleagues. . . . One room? Two rooms?'

'What?' said Anne. 'Two rooms, of course. But who on earth are these people?' she added, turning towards me. 'What is their Psycharium? They are not going to put us in a lunatic asylum, are they ? Is there nothing to be done? Come, do speak to them, Pierre.'

'Gentlemen,' I began. . . . But I felt a recurrence of that fearful timidity of which I had been cured for two months by being alone with one companion. Routchko signed to me to be silent with a wave of his hand, smiled with a forbearance I felt to be infinitely contemptuous,

26

then speaking over our heads, and as if Anne
and I did not exist. 'Two rooms,' he said to
Martin in a sweet and firm voice. 'But you saw
the violence of the reaction? These poor people believe in reality with a fanaticism! Call
a Beos, will you, dear friend?'

Martin pressed a bell and a man in uniform
appeared.

'You are to conduct these two foreigners to
the Psycharium,' said Martin. 'I shall have di-
rect instructions given to Mrs. Alexander.'

The man saluted, then leant over to Martin
and murmured a few words in his ear.

'Ah, yes, that's true,' said Martin. 'I was forgetting the expert. . . . Show him in.'

Anne took my hand. 'But, Pierre, do something or other, I beg you. . . . These people
think we are mad, or are mad themselves. . . .
They have just spoken of an expert. We shall
find ourselves shut up, all of a sudden. . . .
Pierre, you know I am calm, that I can be brave,
but at this moment I am frightened.'

Snake looked at her, and made a sign to Martin.

'Prodigious!' said Martin. 'Fear . . . I haven't
seen that for thirty years.' And he ended by

saying, as if he had been at the theatre: '*Great* talent.'

A door was opened, and a man with a beard, dressed in a sort of smock blotched with colour, came in.

'Good day, Augustus,' said Martin. 'I am sending these two friends of ours to the Psycharium, and I need your visa.'

The man, closing an eye, looked at Anne and me.

'She,' said he. 'Without any doubt . . . charming . . . a skin which takes the light well. . . . Perhaps a little too much in the English style for my taste, but it's not a matter of my taste. . . . Him . . . not so good . . . not nearly so good . . . but peculiar . . . fine curves . . . [With his thumb he outlined the shapes of my cheeks and of my chin in the air.] Yes, that's all right. I'll take them, both of them.'

Martin asked us to stand up.

'Sir,' said Anne to Routchko, 'you look a very good man. Promise me that no harm will be done to us.'

'I promise,' said Routchko, taking her hands. 'I promise that we shall save you from yourselves.'

28

V

OUR guide walked fast. We felt that strange sensation of instability that the solid earth gives to those who have just spent several weeks on board a boat.

The town was strange. It was elegant and flowery, like some of the new cities in Morocco, but extraordinary shapes which exhausted one's emotions and one's eyes had been sought after.

On our way we read with surprise the names of the streets: 'Flaubert Street, Rossetti Park, Proust Avenue, Eupalinos Gardens, Babbitt Square, Baring Terrace, Forster Street.'

'How cultivated these people are,' said Anne. 'It's like walking through a library.'

We tried to cross-question our companion; he spoke English, but obviously did not wish to enlighten us. 'The gentlemen gave me no orders. Mrs. Alexander will explain things to you, she is used to it,' he replied to all our questions.

Moreover, a moment later he pointed out to us a building which looked like a big hotel, at the far end of a square, and said:

'Central Psycharium.'

It was our future residence. A garden surrounded it filled with groups of palm trees and blocks of violet-coloured flowers.

'What is this Ritz of the Pacific, Anne?'

'Some lunatic asylums,' she said, 'are made to look beautiful to cheer the inmates.'

Inside, this Psycharium looked both like a hospital and a museum. Everything in it was labelled. Everywhere one saw time-tables, plans, arrows pointing. 'Permitted Subjects, Reserved Subjects, Novelists' Visiting Hours, Painters' and Sculptors' Visiting Hours.' After a word from the man who had brought us there, the porter rang a bell with an agreeable musical note, three times, and said:

'Mrs. Alexander will come down.'

Mrs. Alexander was a woman who must once have been beautiful. In type she was a curious mixture of English and Tahitian. She was sympathetic at once. Although she had the grave and deferential manners of the better sort of housekeeper, one could see hidden behind this façade a sort of amused impatience which gave a great deal of life to what she said.

'I received your descriptions by telephone,' said she, 'and for once the gentlemen have been precise, so that everything is already prepared. Would you like to see your rooms?'

'We should like above all things to understand,' said Anne.

'You are going to understand,' said Mrs. Alexander, smiling, 'but first we must see the rooms.'

A lift took us to the third floor. Mrs. Alexander went down a long corridor, opened a door, and we were enchanted. I had never seen a pleasanter room. The softness of the colouring (grey and parma violet), the restrained shape of the furniture, the vague tints of the walls, seemed so much designed to suit Anne's taste as I had learned to know it, that I could not prevent myself from telling her so.

'It was Mr. Snake himself who chose the room for you,' said our hostess.

She went to open a window; from a broad balcony, sheltered by a sun-blind, one looked out on a bluish green lake surrounded by the frail silhouettes of leaning coconut palms. In the distance the Peak of Maiana rose up, a pur-

31

ple black mass against the vivid indigo of the sky.

'It is too beautiful,' said Anne, enchanted; 'but who is offering us all this? What is being asked of us in exchange? Are we free?'

'Absolutely free, Madame; the only condition is that you must be at the gentlemen's disposal during visiting hours. Besides, Maiana is an island . . . where would you go?'

'But who are *the gentlemen?*' I asked. 'Ever since we set foot in your territories we have been unable to obtain an explanation. People seem to take pleasure in making us live in an atmosphere of mystery. We have been told several times, Madame, that it would be you who would finally enlighten us. We implore you to speak.'

'Most willingly,' she said. 'But won't you first of all take a bath and change your clothes? . . . Your room, Sir, is this one on the right. Your two bathrooms are next door. . . .'

'No, no,' said Anne, 'we want to know the truth. Who are the Articoles? What is Maiana? What is the Psycharium? What is going to become of us? I'm not a person who can live in uncertainty.'

'Then listen,' said Mrs. Alexander, shutting the

window and offering us arm-chairs. 'But above all remain quite calm; you are not in any danger. Quite the contrary. . . . You are going to pass a few weeks here, after which you will continue your voyage. . . . No more than that. . . . Well, then. . . . Do you remember the English novelist, Anthony Scott, who was famous between 1840 and 1860, made an immense fortune with a bad book, *The Dark Sex,* and then disappeared from the literary world?'

'I know the name of the author and the title of the book,' said Anne, 'but I have never read *The Dark Sex* nor any other of Scott's novels.'

'So much the better for you,' said Mrs. Alexander. 'But did you know that this man Scott, in 1861, bought the island of Maiana outright, from the Dutch Government, with sovereign rights?'

'Wait a moment,' I said. 'I rather think I once read that story. Didn't he introduce a certain number of other writers to keep him company?'

'Precisely. He offered land free to any artist, either writer, painter or sculptor, who would engage never to leave the island and to accept its laws. Forty-three colonists followed him and formed the first generation of Articoles. With them were about three times the number of servants, men and women. It was from them that the other class of the population was formed; which you have heard called the Beos —an abbreviation of the word Beotian which Scott used to call them by. Finally, there was the indigenous population of the island, not numerous, but very good-looking; they married into the Beos to such an extent that to-day, after seventy years, there are no longer any pure natives. All the inhabitants of the island are either Articoles or Beos; they now amount to nearly ten thousand, of which six hundred are Articoles.'

'But what is the difference between the Articoles and the Beos? Only their origin?'

'Oh no! Not at all! Here birth doesn't count; it is what you work at which decides what caste you belong to. The Articoles are purely artistic in function. They write, they paint, they compose music; they cannot follow any trade, not even the book trade, for fear of being prosecuted. An Articole may not possess money.'

'But how does he live?'

Young Beos girls are there to wait on them.

'He lives, thanks to the Beos. I should tell you that many of them have acquired large fortunes. The island is very rich in natural resources. It contains rubber plantations and mines. It has no military expenses since its independence is guaranteed by all the Powers. Whoever wishes to work here quickly acquires great wealth. But the only pleasure of the rich Beos, and especially of his wife and daughters, is to support the Articoles. Every evening, between five and seven o'clock, you may see in the houses of the Beos planters, tables loaded with cakes and sweets, and meat and drink, in front of which the Articoles make their appearance for a few minutes. Young Beos girls are there to wait on them, and in exchange pick up the few words that the Articoles let fall . . . when the gentlemen are able to speak at all.'

It seemed to both of us that there was in Mrs. Alexander's apparently very respectful tone an imperceptible shade of sarcasm, but we were so astonished and so interested by everything which she had just told us that we only thought of asking her further questions.

'Could we be present at one of the Articoles' meals?' I asked.

36

'You will certainly be invited to them yourselves,' she said. 'As soon as the gentlemen have
begun to talk about you, you will be very popu-
lar in the island. The patients at the Psycharium are always sought after by the Beos.'

'But the Psycharium?' asked Anne; 'you must
explain the Psycharium to us.'

'That is easy,' said Mrs. Alexander. 'At first
the Articoles who came from Europe or America, and who had mixed in a complex society,
had a thousand subjects with which to deal; it
was enough for them to delve into their memories to find there the material for their books.
Even the second generation found itself much
less well provided. There were, of course, what
we called here "Maianan themes." The life of
the Beos, the love affairs of Beos women and
Articoles, or of an Articole woman and a Beos.
But that was soon exhausted. Then the Articoles
started writing about one another, but this
caused offence and made things awkward for
many of them. Besides which they had long
ceased having any real feelings, and found nothing more to observe either in themselves or in
their fellows. Some dealt with those secondary
feelings which may be aroused by works of art.

37

For instance, after a voyage like yours, if you were an Articole, you would not only publish your "Journal Aboard," but also your "Journal of that Journal Aboard," and your companion would publish "The Journal of my Husband's Journal Aboard." There is still a rich vein there. The great literary success this year in Maiana is a Confession of sixteen thousand nine hundred pages, written by Routchko, with the title: "Why I cannot write." . . . But after all not every one has Routchko's talent, and it was for the sake of the Articoles in need of characters that a rich Beos landowner who died ten years ago created the Psycharium, which is in essence a collection of human souls. The Psycharium has corresponding members in Europe and America who send it out interesting specimens. Sometimes we happen to find them among the Beos. Sometimes a lucky chance sends us guests like you. . . . The gentlemen try as far as possible to collect here specimens illustrating all the most important feelings which existed in the old romantic societies.'

'What do you call a romantic society, Madame?'

'One in which every one isn't writing romances,' said Mrs. Alexander ingenuously.

Anne and I looked at each other.

'But you, Madam, what are you?' asked Anne. 'An Articole or a Beos?'

'Oh! I?' said Mrs. Alexander. 'I was a Beos by birth and then for twenty-five years the wife of an Articole. I know them well.'

VI

IF Anne and I had not felt a slight feeling of regret when we thought that our fine record was being interrupted, our stay in Maiana would have been a happy one, at least at the beginning.

The natural scenery was beautiful, the climate perfect, we were treated with courtesy. Mrs. Alexander, of whom we had made a friend, had given us the use of a bathing shed, built on the edge of the lake, and we were able to dive off our own terrace—a priceless joy for Anne, who was never happy except in the water. It was delicious swimming in the warm lake, at the bottom of which one could see brilliantly coloured and strangely shaped fishes moving about; it was exquisite, too, to walk through the country, followed by a boy whom, if one was thirsty, one sent swarming to the top of a coconut palm, from which he rained down gigantic nuts full of excellent milk. But we found our chief pleasure in observing the behaviour of the inhabitants.

We never tired of pointing out to each other the examples of the almost comic veneration in which the Articoles were held by the Beos. Some among them carried their fetichism to such a point that they collected any scrap of paper touched by their sacred pens. I have seen one of the richest of the Beos proudly show off an old penholder which had belonged to Routchko, and which he had bought very dear at the Maiana curiosity shop.

To him it was like a sacred relic, and if I had to give a brief sketch of the attitude of the people of Maiana to art and artists, the words I should have to employ would be: religion and priest.

The best of the Articoles are saints who live in the unreal kingdoms of their imagination and who desire nothing in the world except to produce perfect works of art. Their ambition is to imitate the lives of those great and legendary Articoles who are worshipped at Maiana, such as Flaubert, whose bust a great many Beos have in their houses; Shelley, to whom they have erected a sort of temple in which there is a marble statue of him naked; Marcel Proust, from

41

whose works a few pages are read aloud in the theatre on each anniversary of his birth.

The most respected of all living Articoles is Alberti, who has spent his life preparing himself for writing a poem of thirty lines, which he conceived at the age of eighteen and which he has just completed at the age of seventy-two. What adds to the ritual nature of artistic life at Maiana is that it is obligatory. Once a week there is a play at the theatre, or a concert in the giant auditorium. These performances are free and are in the nature of public festivals. The first rows of stalls are reserved for the Articoles and all the Beos have to attend. There is no penal law enforcing it, but social pressure is enough. A Beos convicted of caring for neither music nor letters becomes a sort of pariah. The Articoles give up coming to eat his food; the other Beos despise him; in the end his wife almost always gets him at least to make a show of the respect he does not feel.

The mysteries of art are respected exactly as the mysteries of religion are in other countries. The most celebrated dramatic author in Maiana is Pedro Sanzoni, whose plays are beautiful but so obscure that most of the Beos do not under-

42

stand them, but they only admire Sanzoni the more because of that. Thus it happened that we witnessed during our stay in Maiana an episode which seemed to us a good symbol of the attitude of the Beos.

Sanzoni's favourite actress, Noëmi, was so temperamental a performer that directly she began to play any part, she fell into a sort of trance. To help her get into this nervous condition, necessary to her talent, she insisted that her dresser should put up over the door of her dressing-room, not her own name, Noëmi, but that of the character she was going to play. On a first night, the dresser having forgotten to change the names, Noëmi came on the stage dressed and made up for a part which did not belong to the play. When the other actors heard her delivering meaningless replies they tried to attract her attention, and make her understand her mistake. But Noëmi seemed not to see them. Pedro Sanzoni, in terror, was about to leap on to the stage and stop the performance, when, looking at the spectators, he saw that nothing had disturbed their calm.

He let the act finish. The curtain fell amidst applause from the Beos, who were telling each other that Sanzoni had never written anything more daring.

The censorship of the Articoles forbade the publication of accounts of this episode in the *Gazette;* the play was printed as it had been performed, substituting the incoherent part for the part in the original text, and Sanzoni gave it the new title of 'A Person from Another World.' It has become a Maianian classic. Anne and I heard the true story from Mrs. Alexander. I should add, for the sake of accuracy, that we had liked the play.

It was Mrs. Alexander, too, who had explained to us that during the last few years a dangerous fashion had arisen among some of the younger and more rebellious Beos of openly denying the importance of the Articoles and of regarding them as parasites, and of wishing to rid the island of them, or at all events to take away their privileges and force them to work with their hands. These young people have found a doctrinaire, a degenerate Articole, called Sam Fogg, who teaches his disciples that life is more important than art. These young people are called the Biophiles. They are despised and regarded as immoral persons by the general public; their doctrines spread very little, for marriage almost always brings them back from their aberration into normal life.

Naturally it very often happens that a real Articole is born amongst the Beos. Most of the third generation of Articoles are born Beos. At the Psycharium there is a special department, a sort of seminary, for placing such cases under observation. The practical advantages of an Articole's position are so obvious that cases of a pretended vocation might arise.

And indeed it would be too much to say that they escape this danger altogether in Maiana, but the directors of the seminary do their best. The moment it is a question of their calling the Articoles are admirably honest. I might perhaps reproach them with too great indulgence towards some sham artists, who find it convenient to be fed by the Beos. But the life of a genuine Articole is very hard; the period of creation seems as painful as childbirth; the moments of respite between bouts of creative activity are times of anxiety and of searching. They are almost all of feeble constitution and the importunate hospitality of the Beos exhausts their stomachs. In truth I believe that for the majority of them life would be unendurable but for the devotion of the Beos women.

It is very rare indeed that an Articole chooses an Articole woman as his helpmate. Experience has shown that such marriages almost always turn out badly. But the law in Maiana gives an Articole a first claim on any Beos woman whom he declares under oath to be necessary to his work.

Thus the law of the island allows for temporary unions between Articoles and Beos, unions which do not annul any previously contracted Beos marriage, but provisionally suspend its operation as regards the presumption of paternity.

This is a very ingenious solution of the problem which gets rid of some of the unpleasantness of clandestine adultery; it might perhaps be desirable to introduce it among ourselves. As for the Beos husband, he looks on such a choice as a great honour, he knows that his name will appear in the *Lives of the Articoles* which are published after the death of each one and paid for by the state, and he makes up in social prestige what he loses in conjugal fidelity.

To tell the whole truth, I should add that I

46

have heard some Articoles complain of the privileges thus permitted to them: they contend that the whole literary value of love comes from the difficulties met with in its pursuit. I must admit that the only good novels I read at Maiana were written by men who had once been Beos; this might tend to confirm the theory.

The great weakness of the Articoles seemed to me to be that they have lost contact with life. In a normal state of society, the artist, at least in his youth, has to struggle; he preserves his memories of things, his loves, his hates, in short, his strong feelings. In Maiana an Articole meets with nothing to oppose him in his life. From that springs an incredible ignorance. My readers would not believe me if I quoted some of the questions put to Anne and to me by the most intelligent Articoles.

'I have to describe in my new book,' one of them said to me, 'a mountainous frontier region which smugglers are crossing. But how does one cross a mountain? Are there any paths on it, or roads?'

Another questioned me for a long while about boats; he could not understand how the rudder, oars and sails worked. All questions of ways

47

and means are foreign to them since the Beos take such things off their hands.

Only old Alberti has seen a lot of things in the long period he spent without writing. To an Articole the only real thing is the work of art at which he labours; everything else, what we call reality, is to him a sort of game preserve, or stew for fish, where he goes to look for anything he needs for his spiritual nourishment. The result is that, though I have often taken great pleasure in the conversation of the Articoles, I cannot say that their friendship ever quite satisfied me. I always have the feeling that they are gazing through me, at imaginary beings. In the course of a talk they suddenly lose the thread, and one finds them flying around a hundred feet over one's head.

Their emotional life is always shaped by the life of the work they are creating. If an Articole leaves his mistress, you may be sure he needs a scene of breaking off relations. If he deceives his wife, it is because he must have a jealous scene. I have often been staggered by hearing old men with white hair and innocent eyes say to me: 'I must have a little girl, an incest, a crime.' It is for that reason almost all the

48

Articoles lead such complicated lives; many of them would be chaste and faithful by nature if they did not need for their work the excitement which an acute desire gives to the brain. Routchko, himself, although at the moment when we knew him he was very ill, could not do without a whole court of young Beos girls around him, with whom he carried on almost metaphysical flirtations.

But if the sentimental life of Maiana is complicated, political life is simple there. The Articoles refuse to attend to it, and the administration of the island is delegated to a Commission of Beos. The only supervision which the Articoles exercise is over public spectacles, publications and immigration. The only newspaper on the island, *The Articoles' Gazette,* publishes nothing but details about the works of art in progress and news of the moral and physical health of the principal Articoles. I read, for instance, on the day we entered the Psycharium, a long article on 'Routchko's Asthma.' The following week the *Gazette* began a series of articles, which gave great pleasure, on the Articoles' dreams. Though they have abandoned politics the Articoles are interested in certain questions

49

to do with the urban police, particularly in those regulations the object of which is to enforce silence.

In the quarter inhabited by the masters of Maiana all the roads are covered over with a soft rubber substance, which deadens the noise of carriages. It is forbidden to make use of warning signals, and even to speak in the street, except at meal-times, unless in a low voice. Anne, though her voice is soft, found herself being had up by a policeman of the literary brigade, for having said aloud, 'That is Alberti's house.' Fortunately, these extraordinary sounds attracted Alberti himself to the window of his house and he disposed of the incident. The use of the telephone is forbidden in Maiana between nine o'clock in the morning and midday. For some of the still more nervous Articoles the government has had a Tower of Silence built, in which the rooms, lined with cork, float on a bath of oil. It is forbidden to go within four hundred yards of this tower, to which only special servants have access at fixed hours. Beos women who marry Articoles make a stay at the Tower of Silence before their marriage, and there they undergo a progressive training.

It is forbidden to make use of warning signals, and even to speak in the street, except at meal-times.

Anne thought that many of the Articoles ought to have gone through this school, for though the customs of the island interested us, and though we had nothing but praise for the treatment we received at the Psycharium, yet we suffered from the daily visits, which we were unable to avoid.

VII

Routchko had become attached to me. He had asked me my father's name, always called me Pierre Ivanovitch, and came every morning to spend a few hours with me. On my side I felt affection for him. Two more different characters could not be imagined: I was cold and rebelled at expressing my deep feelings, Routchko was incapable of containing his. He lived with his soul stripped bare before the eyes of anyone who became his friend. It was an attitude I could not adopt, but I respected it and it interested me. He was the purest specimen of the Articoles I have known: nothing counted for him except his own work, and that of his friends. It is true that at the time when I met him he was slowly dying of a disease of the lungs, and that he knew it, but Germain Martin, who had known him in his youth, told me that he had always been the same. Routchko's great sorrow

53

was that I did not write. In his eyes a life devoted to anything except art was a life spoiled; with only a few months to live he felt himself richer than I was:—young and strong, but full of projects for doing things, which in his eyes were nothing, and like a living death. I believe that he ended by saying to himself that the only way of 'awakening me' was to make me talk of Anne, and to force me to reflect on my relations with her. I have seen him irritated into showing contempt—he who was such a gentle character—when the course of conversation led me to declare to him that the longer the voyage had lasted, the more simple and fraternal had my feelings for Anne become; there was in that a moral and physical balance which put him literally into a fury. I, who knew well how I had struggled to attain to it, believed this balance to be a virtue and was proud of it. He was incapable of it and despised it. 'No, no,' he said, taking my hands and gazing at me. 'No, Pierre Ivanovitch, you are not telling the truth. You are lying to yourself, you avoid looking at your deepest self. I know very well, yes, I do, that this frivolity with which you cloak yourself is only an affectation, and that you are worthy of an inner life.'

When he left me I always suffered from a feeling of shame, and of insufficiency, but I could never succeed in finding out whether this feeling was due to the mediocrity of my own poor existence, or to Routchko's morbid confessions.

Sometimes on leaving me he went to see Anne and explained his ideas about me to her.

'What is so awful in the case of Pierre Ivanovitch,' he said to her, 'is that in him pride takes the form of a sense of honour in which he wraps himself and which stifles his real feelings. Don't you see, Anne Mikhailovna, men feel fear of prison, of iron bars, of jailers, and they don't see that they shut themselves up in a prison of words which is a hundred times more close. In a prison cell one can still be oneself. I see further that in a prison cell it is easy to be oneself, but the soul is a dead soul on which has been thrust the extinguisher called honour, the extinguisher called morality, or the even straiter one called good behaviour and knowledge of the world.

'Thus Pierre becomes shut up, proud, he succeeds in appearing poor, he who on the contrary is so rich. . . . It is appalling.'

Then he took Anne's hands, and said to her:
'Anne Mikhailovna, I beg you, help me to save
him.'

'But from what?' asked Anne.

'We must make him face his real self, which
he is slowly murdering. . . . At this moment he
denies his own existence, he walls himself up.
. . . He is playing, I don't know what theatrical
part. . . .'

This continual analysis which Routchko cease-
lessly practised on other people, just as he did on
himself, was so contagious that Anne began to
cross-examine me. She, who had formerly been
so simple, and so matter-of-fact, no longer accepted any words of mine as the expression of
my thoughts. She tried to prove to me that I
had said something or other because I thought
something else which was just the opposite.
Thus life became hateful. I even came to look at
myself in the glass and ask myself: 'But is it true
that I am not really myself?' I was beginning
to believe it. From the fourth week of my stay
in Maiana, I began to keep a diary of my
thoughts, in imitation of the Articoles. I have
this diary before my eyes at this moment; it is a
little notebook, yellow with sea water. I quote

some notes from it because they show the state of anxiety in which I was living then.

2nd July. Am very depressed. Ask myself if Routchko isn't right, if I am not going to pass my life playing a part which isn't my own. Why is it that I act as I do? Why this voyage? Why go back to France? I don't care for glory, or notoriety. . . . Is it, as Routchko says, in order to escape from myself?

3rd July. Another conversation with Routchko. He is right, it is to escape from myself. But to escape from what? And if I were to let all this surface agitation die down, what is the real Ego which I should find under all this? Would it not be emptiness, nothingness, silence? Am I anything besides my words and gesticulations?

4th July. Paddled all day in the lake, and towards evening climbed up the peak. Feel better. Doing things, walking, my body strong and tired.

5th July. I, I, I. But what am I? Are the palm trees, the sea, the distant cape, the paper on which I write, part of me? If one gets rid of that, what remains? It occurs to me now, in thinking of that storm, to be afraid. I might have died, died before having really lived. . . .

6th July. Apologia pro vita mea. I have not lived, I am not living now, I shall never live.

7th July. I am deeply unhappy.

8th July. In spite of myself and calling myself a simpleton, I am beginning a prose poem, in imitation of Snake's manner.

'The boat climbs again up the slope of the wave,
Standing up like a train on the mountain-side.
It falls again with a sound of splintering wood.
In the troughs, too narrow, between the sum-
    mits—
And I, I'm thinking: "Oh, My God, if ever . . .
I am sure that we shall be pooped. . . .
I shall ask him to give me, before my death,
A kiss that shall taste of the salt sea water.
After which most willingly will I die.
For we must die to-day or to-morrow."

Look here, I am going mad. Maiana doesn't suit me. Pierre Chambrelan, *pull yourself to-gether*.

9th July. I was unable to resist the unhealthy desire of showing the beginning of my poem to

Routchko and asking his judgment of it. He did not seem very enthusiastic, and what is seroius is, that this wounded my feelings. Am I becoming an Articole? On the other hand, he was interested for much too long a time over what he calls 'the revealing side of it.' Articoles always want to see in other people's works a novel that they make up while listening.

10th July. Routchko has brought me (is it indirect criticism, or a model?) a poem of Snake's *Libido.* I can remember four lines of it.

'As never fool for love, I starved for you;
My throat was dry and my eyes hot to see.
Your mouth so lying was most heaven in view,
And your remembered smell most agony.'

Obviously it is good, but it seems to me that I could have written that. I asked Routchko if Snake had written these lines a long time ago. 'No,' he replied, 'last week.' After Routchko had gone I went for a long walk by the edge of the lake. How tired I am of this sunlight, of these gilded fish, these coconut palms! How quickly one tires of the most beautiful sights in nature! Either complete stillness or perpetual movement, Buddha or Paul Morand, these are the only paths to happiness.

Copying a few passages of that diary has just called up in my mind the state of melancholy which I was in at that time. In spite of the extraordinary beauty of the place, in spite of the softness of the climate and the charm of the inhabitants, yes, I was unhappy at Maiana, and I was much more so because Germain Martin seemed to take a strange pleasure in tormenting me. He came to visit me every other day, and seemed to have determined to make me jealous of Snake. Nor would he, either, admit that I was not in love with Anne.

'I am a little anxious about my young friend Snake,' he said to me in his beautiful, slow and slightly jarring voice. 'He sees a great deal of your charming neighbour and last night he spoke about her to me in a way which I did not at all like. Moreover, he is working less, and working badly; the two last poems which he showed me are brutal and sensual in expression, quite unworthy of such a great Maianian poet as Snake.'

'You have often told me, Monsieur Martin, that Snake is an ethereal being. No doubt he takes pleasure in fluttering round Anne in this way; it is not dangerous either for him or for her. . . . Snake is much more a spirit than a man.'

'Ye-s,' replied Martin, 'ye-s, but when it is applied to a human being the word "ethereal" must never be taken in too literal a sense. I remember conversations which Snake and I used to have on the subject of sensual love, in which he showed a knowledge of the subject which really astonished me in such a young man. However, if you feel happy about it, it is all right. It was only on your account that I was anxious, because, as far as Snake goes, if he wanted her too badly, the laws of Maiana would give him your travelling companion. A foreign woman is the same as a Beos, so far as Articole marriage is concerned.'

'What?' I asked him. 'I don't understand. You wouldn't give him Anne against her will? That would be behaving like savages.'

'My dear fellow! All the same, you don't believe that we should let a mere mortal woman, by a long-drawn-out resistance, prevent the creation of a masterpiece. . . . Of course, there must be a period of waiting, nothing is more

61

favourable to the birth of sharp emotion, but we shouldn't permit desire to go so far as to become an obsession.'

I do not remember exactly what I replied, but it was certainly a passionate, rather incoherent entreaty.

He watched me silently, and then fell to laughing with a most devilish laughter.

'Most . . . interesting,' he said.

VIII

THE sun was resplendent, the sea violet, the flowers in the garden of the Psycharium perfect, but Maiana had become hateful. I felt that I was becoming bogged in the quagmires of analysis, that I was becoming like the worst of the Articoles, that my life was no more than a perpetual brooding about myself which was slowly poisoning me. It was the same with Anne; she had lost the brilliant colour she had during our passage, seemed in a fever, and wilted away under one's eyes. We had got to fly.

Almost every morning I went down to the port to see if they were working on our boat. A Beos carpenter was slowly putting in new planks, and fitting a bowsprit, but when I asked him if he would soon have finished, he seemed embarrassed, and told me that 'the gentlemen' had given him no orders.

My poor friend Routchko could only breathe

with difficulty; directly he lay down and tried to go to sleep he almost suffocated. The doctors said he could live a week like this or ten days at most. All Maiana was respectfully watching the death-struggle; and it was indeed an heroic spectacle. Routchko spent his last hours in dictating (for he could no longer write) notes on his illness. It was called 'The Death of Routchko.' I heard several fragments of it during the visits I paid him, and I do not think I know of anything more beautiful. Each bout of suffering was described with astonishing clearness of mind and sureness of form. Death is no longer the strange thing it was since I have heard this account of it; it is as familiar to my imagination as love is, or as a hurricane. As our friend wanted to devote all his forces to this last work, he shut his eyes and paid attention only to the internal workings of his body which was breaking up. It was most moving to tiptoe into the room where all the greatest of the Articoles were standing silent, in a ring about the dying man, who lay with his eyes already shut, while young Beos girls caught every murmur of the voice which grew feebler and yet more feeble still. It was then I understood the grandeur that there

Routchko spent his last hours in dictating notes on his illness.

is in the standpoint of the Articoles, in spite of all their weaknesses.

But this was not the only tragedy in this nightmare existence. While Routchko lay on his death-bed, the charming Snake was going mad. At least he became so in the sense in which the Articoles used the word, and which seemed to me myself so odd, that I feel rather at a loss to make the reader understand it. He must remind himself that an Articole in a normal condition thinks of the living world as a dream, and of the world of art as reality. Should a reversal of these values take place, should an Articole when ill begin to think of life as real and important, to such an extent as to neglect his art, the doctors of Maiana say that he is mad. Can I make myself understood by saying that madness in Maiana is an hallucination turned inside out? Now this was exactly what was happening to Snake. For some days Martin told me anxiously that Snake had given up working; I did not attach much importance to these remarks, which I thought were inspired by the wish to see me react. But one morning I saw Martin genuinely upset and very gloomy.

'Our poor Snake,' he said to me, 'has got to be

examined to-morrow by specialists in mental diseases, and I am very much afraid that he will be made to take a forced rest of some months in a lunatic asylum. Snake was one of the finest minds in the island and was a great poet. We're wrong, d'you see, we Articoles, in treating these foreigners' visits as an amusement. It is true they enrich us with a few characters, but a great artist creates his characters without models, and the dangers of such visits are much greater than their benefits. . . . Well!'

He tapped me on the shoulder and said with a seriousness which I had never seen in him before:

'Look here, Chambrelan, if ever I preside again over an Immigration Commission I shall never let women come in here. It is all right with our Beos women, who are good docile creatures, who don't set up to meddle in a man's life. . . . But an European woman! An American woman! Exposing the delicate priceless mechanism of an Articole's mind to the coquettishness and sudden moods of these terrible creatures. . . . No, as long as I enjoy any power among the Articoles we shall not try this experiment again. And as for you, my dear friend, you and your female companion, your lover, sister, whatever name you choose to call her by, be off as soon as possible, whenever you like.'

'Are you speaking seriously? Shall we be able to leave?'

'I've had orders given this morning to the Public Works Department of Maiana for your boat to be ready as soon as possible. . . . It will be at the latest in a week's time.'

I must admit that in spite of the sad cause of his veering round like this (the madness of poor charming Snake) I felt myself borne away by matchless bliss. But I was aware that it would be bad taste to reveal it too much.

'Tell me about Snake,' I asked. 'What has happened to him? A crisis?'

'Yes,' said Martin. 'It is like this. I have not concealed from you that for some time past I have seen that Snake was very much in love with your friend. I attached very little importance to this until the day before yesterday. Seeing that he was so remote from his work and noticing that he scarcely replied when one spoke of his poem, I offered to have this woman given to him for three months or for six months, by the Commission on Articole marriages, of which I am

68

the Vice-President. . . . You may imagine my surprise when he flatly refused.'

'He refused,' I said joyfully.

'He refused,' Martin went on with indignation, 'replying that this woman Anne loved you, that she had told him so, and that he did not wish to have her except by her own free will. In face of such an hallucination it was my duty to have a doctor called. Unhappily there could be no doubt about the diagnosis: a profound belief in the reality of life, a psychosis of the most dangerous sort. And no doubt to-day he will appear even more deranged to the experts, for since last night he has been raving; he says that a poem is nothing but an arrangement of words, that every artist is a mysterymonger, that one hour of true love is worth all the books in the world—plain madness.'

I must here confess a piece of meanness. It was clear to myself that Snake had never been less mad in his life, but what good would it have served to have said so? The Articoles' minds do not work like ours. In the sense in which an Articole like Martin uses the word 'madness' Snake was mad.

If I open my Maiana diary at that date, the

last on which I confided my secrets to its pages,
I do not find one word about Snake's condition,
but simply this:

'This woman Anne loves you; she told him so.'

IX

Our boat, repainted all over, had been rigged
with large sails of an ochre colour which formed
a pleasant contrast with the glaring blue of the
sea.   At the door of the Psycharium Mrs. Alexander had kissed Anne.   'I must ask your for-
giveness,' she had said to us, 'for having kept you
prisoners for so long, though it was much against
my will."

'You, Mrs. Alexander,' said Anne, 'but you
made our stay delightful. . . .'

'Not too delightful, I hope,' Mrs. Alexander
replied with one of her mysterious sad smiles.   'I
should like, if you ever think of Maiana later on,
that it should be with a spice of terror.   Maiana
must make you love its opposite."

'You know,' said Anne, 'that I have promised
you that.'   They were no doubt alluding to conversations that they had had on this subject and
in which I had not been mixed up.   I walked a

few steps away; they kissed each other once more and Anne came running to overtake me.

Germain Martin had come down as far as the port to bid us farewell. We were genuinely sorry to be leaving him. Though he had played a little on our emotions, his intelligence and his charm made it impossible for us not to forgive him. Alas! our short visit had been long enough to make friendships and to dissolve them. Of the three judges who had met us on that same beach, only one was present at our departure. Anne's eyes were red, perhaps mine were too. Martin, who was too good an Articole for such thoughts (psychosis of the worst sort), seeing us moved, drew out his pocket-book and took a note.

Beos sailors put cases of provisions on board. The Maianians had treated us very generously and we carried away more victuals and water than were needed for our short voyage to Tahiti. Martin preferred to speak of small details; he insisted that the scene of our departure should be composed like a chapter out of one of his own books. At the moment when we said good-bye he said to us:

'Farewell, but write to me and tell me how

the story ends.' We drew away very slowly, rowing, then our sails filled, and we rounded the cape at the end of which was poor Routchko's tomb among the red rocks. On the other side, among the palm trees, the white house with flower-grown balconies was the asylum in which Snake was no doubt dreaming of the too-real face of Anne. The sun sank in a buttercup sky. The sea was faintly rippled, like the surface of a lake broken by a stone.

Little mauve clouds grew pale, and faded away. Above us, the first stars twinkled. Seated on the deck, Anne and I talked for a long while about the Articoles. At this moment, when the calm sea had put a little distance between us and them, we were left with a rather sweet impression of something grand and strange.

'Yes,' I said, 'they are freed from material things, and it is that in truth towards which the efforts of mankind are bent. Other peoples overcome facts by means of magic, religion, or science. The Articoles have taken a road that cuts across. They have got ahead of us.'

'That's true,' said Anne.

'Only I wonder, are they free, or do they only wish to believe they are? And are they happy?'

'That depends. . . . I believe that Routchko was happy.'

'Yes, Routchko was happy because he believed it. . . . All the same, his Journal . . . It seems to me that a really happy man would not feel the need to live twice over like that. . . . Let us say, if you like, Pierre, that Routchko was an unhappy man who knew how to escape from his own unhappiness.'

'Doesn't happiness lie in that?'

'No,' she said, shaking her head with a sort of light-hearted confidence.

'No, I believe that there is such a thing as positive happiness.'

She fell dreaming for a moment, then went on:

'And Snake, would you say that Snake was happy?'

'Until the moment when he met you, very happy. You remember that look he had on the day of our arrival, like a young god? But you brought him to earth. He will have to get over the shock. Then he will take wing once more. Snake will be saved. Martin . . . I'm not so sure. . . .'

'I like Martin very much,' said Anne.

74

'Yes, I do too, but I don't know why.'

She took a deep breath of the warm air and licked her lips.

'Oh, that taste of salt,' she said. Then she came back to the Articoles:

'What about the future? What will become of them? What will Maiana be like in twenty years' time?'

'Who knows? Perhaps all the Beos will have become Articoles and it will be impossible to find anyone to cultivate the ground, to cook, or to do anything. And perhaps the whole island will die of hunger without noticing it.'

'Or perhaps, on the other hand,' said Anne, 'the Beos will rise in revolt, and thinking themselves gulled for too long by an illusion, they will entirely destroy the Articole civilization.'

'Everything is possible, darling Anne, everything is always possible.'

Anne took my arm and she herself put it about her shoulders. The moon in rising woke up the silvery clouds. Tiny waves broke with a gentle murmur on the sides of the *Allen*.

Anne's smell, so delicate, so familiar, was mingled with the perfumes of the night at sea. I thought of poor Snake's poem, 'Your mouth so lying was most heaven in view,' and as I slowly bent down over that mouth I should have been perfectly happy, if I had not had a queer sensation that, hidden in the cracks of the silent night, an immense Articole was spying on us.

(1)

THE END